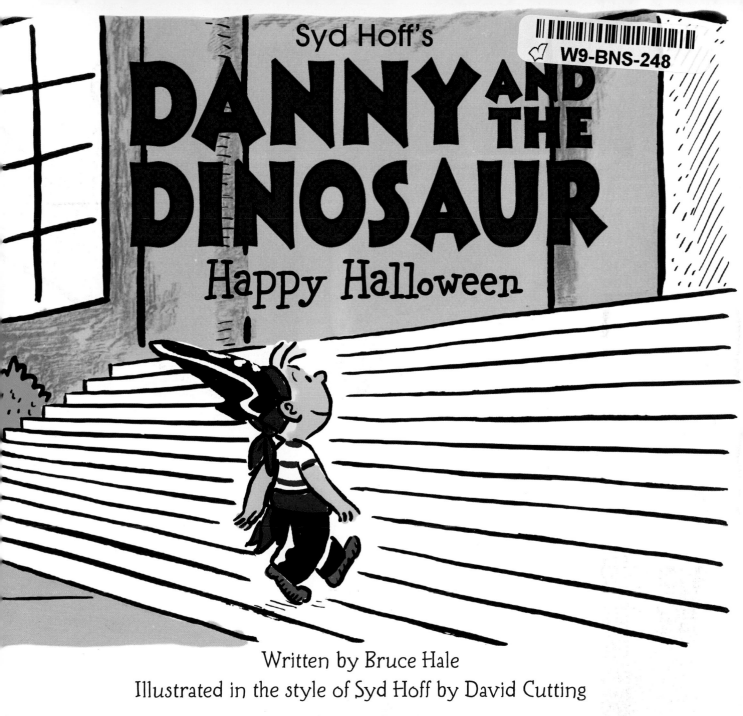

Syd Hoff's

DANNY AND THE DINOSAUR

Happy Halloween

Written by Bruce Hale

Illustrated in the style of Syd Hoff by David Cutting

HARPER FESTIVAL
An Imprint of HarperCollinsPublishers

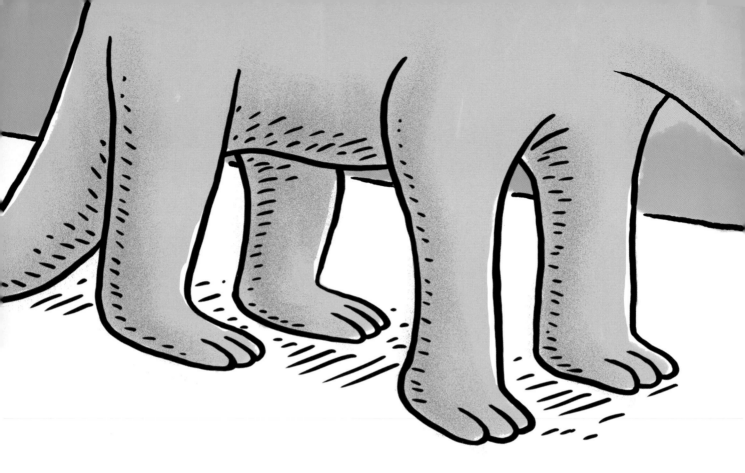

HarperFestival is an imprint of HarperCollins Publishers.

Danny and the Dinosaur: Happy Halloween
Copyright © 2016 by Anti-Defamation League Foundation, Inc.,
The Authors Guild Foundation, Inc., ORT America, Inc., United Negro College Fund, Inc.
All rights reserved. Manufactured in China.
No part of this book may be used or reproduced in any manner whatsoever without
written permission except in the case of brief quotations embodied in critical articles and reviews.
For information address HarperCollins Children's Books, a division of HarperCollins Publishers,
195 Broadway, New York, NY 10007.
www.harpercollinschildrens.com

Library of Congress Control Number: 2015938889
ISBN 978-0-06-241043-6
Book design by Jeff Shake
16 17 18 19 20   SCP   10 9 8 7 6 5 4 3 2 1
❖
First Edition

Danny was excited. "Tonight is Halloween, and I can't wait! It'll be so much fun!"

"Absolutely!" said Danny's friend the dinosaur. "What's Halloween?"

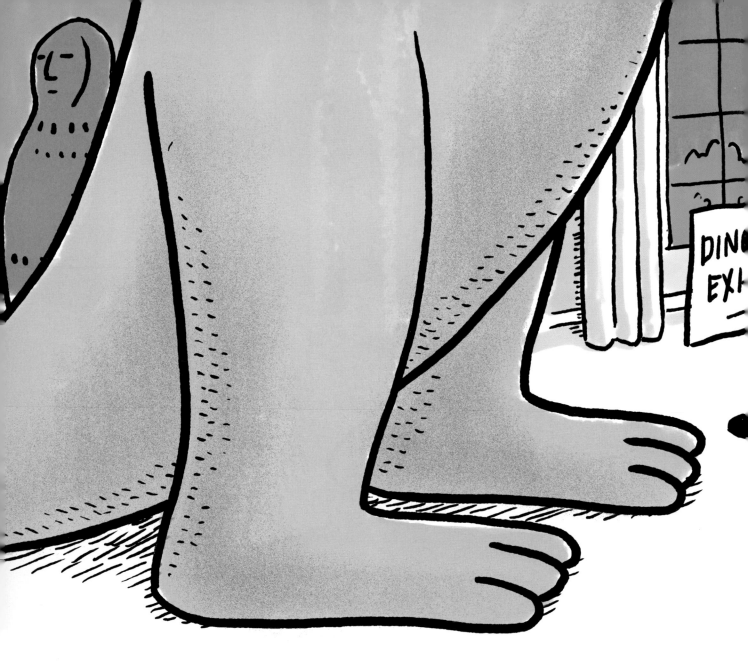

"Everyone wears spooky costumes," said Danny. "You go trick-or-treating from house to house. And people give you candy!"

"That does sound fun," said the dinosaur. "Can I go trick-or-treating?"
"Sure," said Danny. "But first, you need a costume."

They tried on some costumes.

A knight? Not quite.

A cowboy? Nope.

A mummy?
Not so much.

"Nothing works!" said the dinosaur.

"I know," said Danny. "You can be a ghost!"

And with a few adjustments here and there, they were ready for trick-or-treating.

"Great costume!" shouted the other kids.
"Thanks," said the dinosaur.
"I'm a ghost-asaurus."

"Trick or treat!" said Danny and the dinosaur.
"Aren't you a little old for trick-or-treating?" asked the lady.
"Not me," said the dinosaur. "I'm only a hundred million years old."

Sometimes the trick-or-treating got a little tricky . . .

HARPER FESTIVAL
An Imprint of HarperCollinsPublishers

Pumpkin Stencil

HARPER FESTIVAL
An Imprint of HarperCollinsPublishers

... but with a helping hand, Danny and the dinosaur carried it off.

At the end of the night, Danny and the dinosaur had a LOT of candy. "Yum, yum!" said the dinosaur. He gobbled up his treats in two bites, while Danny was just getting started.

"Oops," said the dinosaur. "No more treats." He hung his head sadly.
"Cheer up," said Danny. "I know where we can find more."

He took the dinosaur to a hopping Halloween party. Everyone was laughing and playing games, like Pin the Wart on the Witch, Pumpkin Bowling, and Mummy Wrap.

But the best game of all was bobbing for apples. Thanks to his large mouth, the dinosaur was the best apple-bobber ever!

Soon the dinosaur had a whole PILE of apples.
Danny looked at his candy. He looked at the apples.

"Wow, those look tasty," Danny said.

"Trade you?" said the dinosaur.
"Half of my pile for half of your pile?"

They made the trade. Danny and the dinosaur munched their Halloween treats until they were full enough to pop.

Then they told *spooky* stories all the way back to the museum, scaring each other silly, as friends do.

"Happy Halloween, dinosaur!" said Danny.

"Happy Halloween, Danny!" said the dinosaur. "Thanks to you, my first Halloween was the best ever!"